The *Pocket Cats* series is dedicated to all cat
lovers, everywhere . . . including you!

Pocket Cats

Double Dare

Kitty Wells

David Fickling Books

OXFORD · NEW YORK

31 Beaumont Street
Oxford OX1 2NP, UK

POCKET CATS 7: DOUBLE DARE
A DAVID FICKLING BOOK

978 1 849 92031 5

Published in Great Britain by David Fickling Books,
a division of Random House Children's Books
A Random House Group Company

This edition published 2011

1 3 5 7 9 10 8 6 4 2

Typeset in 16/20 Times by Falcon Oast Graphic Art Ltd.

DAVID FICKLING BOOKS
31 Beaumont Street, Oxford, OX1 2NP

www.kidsatrandomhouse.co.uk
www.rbooks.co.uk

Addresses for companies within The Random House Group Limited can be found at:
www.randomhouse.co.uk/offices.htm

THE RANDOM HOUSE GROUP Limited Reg. No. 954009

A CIP catalogue record for this book is available from the British Library.

Printed and bound in Great Britain by CPI Bookmarque, Croydon.

Chapter One

Maddy Lloyd sat on a swing in the school playground, swaying idly from side to side as she kept an eye on the school building. What was keeping Rachel so long, anyway? Maddy's best friend had stayed behind at break to talk to Mrs Pratt about something, and she'd been gone ages. Break was practically over now!

Blowing out a bored breath, Maddy glanced around the playground . . .

and her gaze fell on Esme Dawson, a new girl with short brown hair gelled into soft spikes. Esme had a grin on her face, and was beckoning the group of girls around her into a tight huddle. "OK, guys," Maddy heard her say. "Here's what we're going to do!" Green eyes glinting, Esme took something out of her pocket and began to whisper.

Double Dare

Maddy's swing slowed down and then stopped as she sat watching. Esme had only started at Henderson Primary a few days ago, when school had begun again after the summer holidays, but already everyone in Class 6A liked her. Maddy could see why. Esme was *really* cool. Apart from her hair, she wore mascara, even though they weren't supposed to wear make-up at school. And she wore a multi-coloured set of stretchy rubber friendship bracelets on her wrist, even though they weren't supposed to wear jewellery either.

Maddy knew she'd be very nervous to start a new school where she didn't know anyone, but Esme didn't seem at all daunted – she'd been laughing and playing pranks from the

moment she'd arrived. On Tuesday,
their second day back, she'd even
sneaked to the front of the classroom
and stuck Mr Orwell's white-board
marker to his desk with Blu-tack!
Maddy hadn't been able to stop
herself from laughing along with the
others at their teacher's startled face
when he tried to pick it up. Even
Mr Orwell had had to laugh – and

ever since then,
Esme had had
a crowd around
her wherever she
went.

Maddy twisted
a strand of her
long brown hair
wistfully around
her finger as she

4

watched Jasmine, Sadie and Mia,
all giggling along with Esme as
she plotted something else. Though
Maddy wouldn't swap her best friend
for anyone, she couldn't help wishing
that she and Rachel could be part of
the group of girls crowded around
Esme too.

Not that that would ever happen.
Maddy made a face. Sometimes she
felt like she was almost invisible, as
far as the rest of 6A was concerned.

"Maddy!" Rachel came running
round the side of the building from
their classroom, her long blonde
ponytail bouncing. "Sorry I'm late,"
she said. Flopping into the swing next
to Maddy, she adjusted her glasses on
her nose. "Guess what – Mrs Pratt's
thinking of starting a science club on

Friday lunchtimes! Wouldn't that be awesome?"

Maddy held back a smile. Rachel was very logical, and loved science – but even so, she was probably the only person in the world who would get excited over a science club. "Oh, *that* sounds like fun," she teased.

Rachel spun in her swing with a

grin, nudging against Maddy. "It
would be! I really hope it happens.
You could join too."

Seeing her friend's eyes gleaming at
the thought, Maddy quickly changed
the subject. "Look, I think Esme's
planning something again," she said,
shooting another glance at Esme's
group. Then she gasped, as all at once
a tingling sensation swept across
her cheeks . . . almost as if she had
whiskers! Remembering the last time
this had happened, Maddy's heartbeat
quickened.

Rachel didn't notice. "She's going
to get into *so* much trouble if she's
not careful," she said, shaking her
head. "Did you see her playing dares
at morning break? She made Mia
and Sadie go out of the gates and

get a conker from the tree across the road. It was really stupid. Any of the teachers could have seen them."

Maddy was hardly listening. She opened her mouth to tell Rachel about the tingling – but then, as quickly as it had come, it vanished again. Disappointment flooded through her. She had been so sure! *I must have just imagined it*, she thought glumly.

"What is it?" said Rachel, seeing her expression.

Maddy told her. "For a second I thought it was the cat magic coming back," she admitted in a low voice.

Rachel squeezed her arm in sympathy. "Has there been any sign of them?" she asked.

Maddy shook her head. "No, they haven't changed since ballet camp

in the summer – and that was over a
month ago."

Both girls sighed. Because, though
no one but Rachel knew it, Maddy
had an incredible secret. On her desk
at home was a set of three small
ceramic cats . . . and every so often,
when there was a problem that needed
solving, one of them would actually
come to life. Though it had already

happened six times, Maddy knew that she'd never get used to having such amazing magic in her life.

At the thought of the cats, suddenly Maddy felt happy again. *So what if Rachel and I aren't part of Esme's gang*, she thought, glancing back at Esme. *Nobody else has magical cats in their bedroom!*

"Ow!" she burst out. There it was again! Her cheeks felt as if they had just been pricked with lots of tiny needles.

Rachel was staring at her. "Maddy?"

"It *is* my whiskers," hissed Maddy, suddenly not having a shadow of a doubt in her mind. "Rachel, the magic's come back, it really has!" Excitement soared through her. The last time one of the cats had come to

life, Maddy had had this exact same tingling. The cats had said that it was her imaginary cats' whiskers, sensing there was a problem that needed magical help.

"Oh, hurrah!" crowed Rachel, squeezing Maddy's arm. "But who has the problem?" she added, staring around them.

Maddy looked too, taking in the

boys climbing on the jungle gym, and the younger children playing football and going down the slide. She turned slowly, but already, deep in the pit of her stomach, she thought she knew what was setting the tingling off.

"It's Esme!" she said in a low voice. As she gazed at the new girl, her 'whiskers' felt as if they were practically vibrating.

Rachel gasped. "Are you sure? What can *Esme* possibly need help with?"

"I don't know. But you know what this means, Rache!"

Rachel's eyes shone as she nodded. "Greykin is going to come to life again."

Maddy felt as if she was sparkling all over. "Maybe he already has!"

* * *

The day seemed to go on for ever.
It was almost impossible to sit still
when Maddy knew that another
adventure was beginning and at home,
Greykin might be roaming around her
bedroom!

Luckily Mr Orwell didn't notice
her fidgeting – his attention was
distracted by Esme's latest trick.
She'd set a stink bomb off, which
meant the whole class had to leave
the classroom and go and work in the
playground.

"These tricks have got to stop,"
Mr Orwell told the class sternly at
the end of the afternoon. "One trick
was funny, two is disruptive. You are
in Year Six now and I expect more
from you. If there are any more jokes

played, the whole class will be in serious trouble."

Maddy glanced across at Esme and saw her nodding, wide-eyed and innocent, as if she agreed with everything the teacher was saying. It was only as he turned away that Esme grinned wickedly at all her friends and gave them a thumbs-up.

She seemed so at ease and popular. Maddy found it hard to believe that the new girl really had a problem that the cats' magic was needed for! But the feeling was clear – whenever Maddy looked at Esme, her cheeks prickled and tingled. She longed to get home and talk to Greykin about it.

Oh, please let him have come to life, she prayed.

As soon as the bell rang and Mr

Orwell said they could go, Maddy
rushed into the cloakroom. Calling
goodbye to Rachel, she grabbed her
coat and charged round to her younger
brother's classroom on the opposite
side of the school building. Jack had
his coat on, but was busy swapping
monster cards with his friends.

"Come on, Jack," Maddy urged.
Now she was in Year Six, her mother
had said that she and Jack could walk
home together on their own. "I want
to go!"

"In a minute," Jack said, barely
looking round.

Maddy fidgeted impatiently.
Outside she could hear mums and
dads and child-minders collecting
children. "Jack!" she appealed.

He finished his swap and ran out

past her. "Why are you keeping me
waiting, Maddy?" he called over his
shoulder with a cheeky grin. "Race
you home!"

Maddy was only too glad to race
after him, her schoolbag bouncing on
her back. She couldn't wait to get to
her bedroom!

Their mum was working in the study on
the computer as they burst in through
the front door in a dead heat. "Hi, you
two," she called out. "There're some
fairy cakes in the kitchen."

"Yay, fairy cakes!" shouted Jack.

"Thanks, Mum – I'll get one in a
minute," Maddy said, kicking off her
shoes and pounding up the stairs.

"What's the rush?" she heard her
mum say in astonishment. But Maddy

was already at the top of the stairs. Bursting into her bedroom, her eyes flew straight to her desk. Her heart leaped. There were only two cats there! Sleek, black Nibs sitting snugly against Ollie, the tabby.

Hearing a purr from her bed, Maddy swung round. A tiny grey cat was sitting on her pillow, no larger than a mouse.

"Greykin!" squealed Maddy. Rushing over, she scooped him up. His small body felt warm and solid in her hands. She held him to her face and he rubbed his cheek against hers, his fur softer than thistledown. "Oh, I've missed you!" she cried.

"And I've missed you," said Greykin, purring loudly as he nudged against her. "It *is* good to be back."

After a while he sat down on Maddy's palm, regarding her with his sparkling golden eyes. "You've been having some interesting adventures, then – just as I promised," he said.

Maddy smiled, remembering the adventure that she and Nibs had had with a dog – much to Nibs's disgust! And her time with Ollie at the English Ballet Academy, only last month. "Oh yes!" she breathed. "It's been amazing."

"I thought it might be," smiled Greykin. He flicked his tail neatly round his paws, a musing look on his broad face. "And now it's time for us to help someone else – but the question is, who?"

"I think I know already!" The words tumbled out of Maddy. "It's this new girl at school – Esme. I felt my cheeks tingling today whenever I looked at her."

She quickly told him all about it. Greykin nodded thoughtfully from her palm. "Yes, it's something to do with that girl, all right – my whiskers are tingling too. Do you have any idea what the problem might be?"

"I don't know. I—" Maddy broke off as her bedroom door opened.

It was her mum with a fairy cake

on a plate. "Talking to yourself?" she chuckled.

Maddy bit her lip. "Er – no, I was just . . ." On her hand, Greykin had instantly transformed back into a cold ceramic cat.

Spotting him, her mum smiled and ruffled Maddy's hair. "Oh, I see – talking to Greykin! I thought I'd better bring you a cake before Jack ate them all." She grinned teasingly. "Maybe Greykin would like one too."

Maddy managed to smile. "Maybe."

"It'll be tea time in an hour – jacket potatoes and tuna tonight," said

Mum. Going out again, she shut the
door behind her.

The moment she was gone, Greykin
turned back to warm, living fur on
Maddy's palm. He shook his head,
looking put out. "Cake indeed.
We cats are carnivores!" He gave
a shudder, gazing at the treat in
distaste. "However, *tuna* on the other
hand . . ."

"I'll bring you some up at tea time,"
Maddy promised. She loved sneaking
Greykin bits of food from the kitchen.
She sat down on the bed and he
jumped onto her knee, his tiny claws
carefully sheathed so as not to prick
her.

"And now, Esme . . ." he said,
pacing around her lap thoughtfully.
"I think I'd better go to school with

you tomorrow and see if I can pick up anything about her."

"Great!" Maddy started to say – and then she frowned doubtfully as she remembered. "Wait, we're going on a school trip tomorrow. To a museum in town."

Greykin's face lit up. "Excellent! I shall enjoy that. History has always been a pet subject of mine." He held his head up proudly as he glanced at the other two cats. "Back when we were in Persia, of course, we three were presented to emperors and kings . . ."

Maddy leaned forward. "When was that, exactly?" she asked. She and Rachel were always trying to find out more about the cats' history, but so far the cats had revealed very little about themselves.

Greykin raised an eyebrow. "Why, it was when we were there, of course."

"Yes, but when? Which year?" Maddy held her breath.

"You know, tuna in an hour sounds all very well and good," Greykin said conversationally. "But would there be any likelihood of a snack? It's been a *very* long time since I last ate." He pressed himself against Maddy's hand and blinked up at her persuasively with his golden eyes.

Maddy sighed and gave up. She knew only too well by now that the cats never talked unless they wanted to!

"I think there's some ham in the fridge – shall we go and see?" Placing the little cat on her shoulder, Maddy hid him under her curtain of long brown hair. "Ready, Greykin?" she asked.

"Oh yes," Greykin purred into her ear. "For anything!"

Chapter Two

"Have you got him with you?" Rachel whispered the next day, as they sat on the coach on the way to the museum.

Maddy nodded. "He's asleep." She looked around, but no one seemed to be paying any attention to them. Across the aisle, Nathan and Ben were having an arm wrestling competition. Gently, Maddy opened her jacket pocket.

Rachel caught her breath as she

saw Greykin curled up nose to tail, his eyes shut, sides moving in and out as he snored softly. "Oh, it's so great to have him back," she breathed.

As Maddy shut her pocket, she suddenly felt the familiar tingling on her cheeks. Looking a few rows back from her and Rachel, she saw Esme and her gang leaning across the aisles, talking and laughing.

"Here, have some strawberry lipgloss," said Esme, handing round a pot. "It makes your lips go all *tiiiiiingly!*" She pulled a funny face and the girls around her grinned, reaching eagerly for the lipgloss.

"So, what are we going to do at the museum, Esme?" Jasmine, who was sitting next to her, asked. She was a tall girl with thick black hair. "Have you got anything fun planned?"

"Ask a silly question!" grinned Esme. "I think it's going to be the perfect place to do some dares."

Sadie and Mia, who were on the opposite side of the aisle, both giggled and started to hand out some sweets. Sadie had shoulder-length blonde hair, and Mia was small and dark.

"We'll stick with each other all the way round," declared Esme. "I bet we'll have loads of fun."

Overhearing, Rachel sighed. "I hope those four aren't going to ruin the day. Mr Orwell will just get really cross if they mess around all the time."

"Mm," answered Maddy. Though she knew Rachel was right, she couldn't help wishing that they were part of the laughing group of girls too. But as she gazed at the back of Esme's spiky head, she realized it was about as likely as finding Greykin tucking into a fairy cake. Girls like Esme never noticed girls like her and Rachel!

Just then Maddy felt Greykin stir. Slipping her hand into her pocket, she stroked his soft fur. His tiny tongue rasped across her fingers, and her pocket shook as he purred. Rachel felt the movement too.

Their eyes met, and Maddy felt a wave of pure happiness. She had Greykin in her pocket and Rachel beside her. So what if she wasn't one of Esme's friends? She was still the luckiest girl in the world!

"Quiet, everyone!" Mr Orwell called, getting them all into a group on the first floor of the museum. He was a new teacher, and it took him ages to get them organized. "Daniel, stop it!" he said, looking anxious as Daniel Bates tried to trip up Nathan. "Now, have you all got clipboards, questionnaires and pens?"

"Yes, sir," a few people muttered.

Everyone else just nodded.

"Boring," Esme whispered behind Maddy and Rachel.

"Right, now I really want you to look carefully at all the displays and exhibits," Mr Orwell said enthusiastically. "Make the most of your time here. Fill in the questionnaires. There will be prizes for those of you who get all the answers right!" He stopped, as if expecting a reaction. But all he got were sighs and rolled eyes.

"Can we go now?" asked Esme.

"Oh, all right. Go on," said Mr Orwell. "But remember, stay on this floor. No going up or down the stairs and . . ." His words were drowned out by the thunder of feet and yells as everyone charged off. Maddy saw him shake his head in despair.

"Come on," said Rachel eagerly. "I want to get all the questions right. Shall we go to the Egyptian section first?"

"But shouldn't we try and stay near Esme?" whispered Maddy. "We've got to find out what the problem is!" And that was true, Maddy told herself . . . but really, she knew that she just wanted to see what Esme and her gang got up to.

"Well, look – she's going that way too," Rachel pointed out.

They followed Esme and her friends into the Egyptian section of the museum: a shadowy room with a curved, cave-like ceiling. There were glass display cabinets with artifacts from Egyptian times, and a big deep

table with a glass top that showed the embalming process. Around the outside of the room were replica mummy cases cordoned off with ropes, a display stand with a vase also behind ropes, and posters showing the different Egyptian gods.

"Ooh, this vase is interesting,"
said Rachel, peering at it. "Look,
it says here it's from the time of
Tutankhamun." Maddy glanced at the
vase, trying to look interested. It was
brown, with paintings of Egyptian
people circling all around it.

Wandering over to the table next,
Rachel started reading all the details.
"Hey, and look at this! It tells you
exactly how they made mummies."

But by now Maddy was too busy
watching Esme and the others. They
were messing about by a spiral
staircase that led to a fire escape.

"What shall I put for question
one?" Jasmine asked, reading her
questionnaire out. "It says, *What is the
name of the mummy in the corner?*"

"I know, put down Mr Orwell!"

Double Dare

Esme giggled. "Oh yes, and look at this question: *who was Ramesses II married to?* I'm going to put Mr Orwell down for that one too!" They all started laughing as she wrote their teacher's name down on her sheet.

Maddy heard Rachel sigh beside her. "That lot are so immature. Have you got the right answers, Maddy?"

"Um – I think so." Maddy quickly started to scribble down the correct answers. But as she did, she kept glancing over at Esme and her friends, who had started daring each

other to do things. They did look like
they were having fun, even if they
were being silly.

Suddenly Maddy felt a tingling
sensation sweep over her . . . as
though her invisible whiskers were
quivering! She blinked. Was the
problem going to happen right now?
She glanced again at Esme and the
others, and felt a sharp pang of envy.
They all looked like they were having
such a great time. What could the
problem possibly be?

Maybe it's a mistake, she thought.

"Hey, do you dare me to go to the
top of the staircase and slide down?"
Esme asked.

"Yeah, go on," urged Jasmine. "I
dare you!"

Esme ran up the staircase as fast

as she could and then slid
down the banister.
"Ha!" she said,
leaping off at the
end. "Now my
turn to make
a dare. Jaz, I
dare you to
go and get
inside the
mummy
case!" The
girls all
shrieked.

"Sssh! Someone will come in if
we make too much noise." Esme
said, her green eyes sparkling. "Go
on, Jasmine."

Maddy was distracted by a
movement in her pocket. *Maddy!*

Greykin's voice came into her head.

Excitement leapt through Maddy as she realized. *Greykin!* she thought back. In her last adventure, she had discovered that her bond with the cats had now become so strong they could talk to her in her head if they needed to.

Quickly, Maddy found a quiet space near the very back of the room where she could concentrate. *What is it?* she thought. A picture of Greykin came into her head. He was sitting bolt upright, his furry face worried.

My whiskers! I can feel them tingling!

Yes, me too, admitted Maddy. *Only I – I thought it might be a mistake, somehow.*

A mistake? echoed Greykin in

amazement. Maddy's cheeks flushed slightly as she realized that she hadn't really wanted to pay much attention to the tingling sensation – she'd been far too engrossed in watching Esme and the others.

I think something's about to happen, Greykin went on grimly. *We have to stop it! Put me on your shoulder and take me closer to Esme. I'll hide under your hair.*

Maddy checked that no one was looking, and then reached into her pocket. Slipping the tiny cat on to her shoulder, she could feel

his little claws digging into her school sweatshirt, and his fur tickling her neck. She went back towards the others. Rachel looked engrossed in the display, still scribbling down notes on her sheet. Jasmine was just scrambling out of the mummy case, looking flushed.

"The Return of the Mummy!" Esme said in a spooky voice, waggling her fingers at Jasmine.

Sadie and Mia cracked up.

"I *want* my mummy!" joked Jasmine with a giggle. "That was seriously weird."

Maddy edged closer. Esme's eyes swept over her, but she didn't even seem to see her.

"Oh yes, the Egyptians," murmured Greykin in Maddy's ear as she

stopped near the posters of the gods
and goddesses. She could feel him
peering out through her hair. "They
certainly knew a thing or two. Did
you know they worshipped cats?" She
heard a note of pride in his voice. "A
very sensible race!"

"Right, next dare! Next dare!" Esme
was declaring eagerly. "Let's make
this a really good one." She glanced
around. "I know! Sadie – I dare you
to take that vase off the stand over
there." The large brown vase was the
same one Rachel had looked at earlier,
and was on a stand that was taller than
the girls.

"I can't do that!" Sadie protested. "I
can't even reach it."

"You can if you stand on tiptoe,"
said Esme.

Sadie shook her head. "No, I can't," she said.

Esme made clucking noises like a chicken.

Sadie put her hands on her hips. "Go on then, *you* do it," she challenged.

Esme grinned. "Ha! I thought you'd never ask."

Maddy felt Greykin go tense. "This is it – I can feel it!" he said in her ear.

Maddy was sure he was right – her cheeks were burning like fire too.

"This is the problem that you have to stop," he said swiftly.

Maddy's heart lurched. As soon as the problem was solved, Greykin would transform back into being just a ceramic cat again. That was the way the magic always worked. But she'd only had a day with him! "It can't be the problem," she whispered. "Not yet."

"It is!" Greykin's claws kneaded her shoulder, catching in her jumper. "I don't know what's going to happen, but be ready, Maddy – ready for anything!"

Chapter Three

As Esme approached the vase, Maddy's heart pounded. She felt dizzy at the thought of the problem occurring so soon. She didn't want to lose Greykin yet.

"Maddy, concentrate!" the little cat warned, seeming to sense her thoughts were wandering. "Oh, what is that girl doing?" he said in dismay as Esme stood on tiptoe, trying to reach the vase. "Remember your cat powers, Maddy. You may need them."

Each cat's magic gave Maddy
special powers, and Greykin's let her
perform amazing athletic feats, so that
she could run and jump and climb
with feline grace and speed. Taking
a breath, Maddy pushed away her
worries about Greykin leaving. She
had to concentrate, or her cat powers
wouldn't work.

Think cat, she thought. *Cat, cat,
cat . . .*

As Esme's hands stretched above
her head, closing on the smooth sides
of the vase, Maddy felt a sparkling,
crackling energy surge through her.
Suddenly she was filled with the urge
to pounce and leap!

"Got it!" Esme cried in glee as she
lifted the vase off the stand. But it was
clearly heavier than she'd thought it

would be. "Wh . . . oa," she gasped as she staggered, holding it above her head.

Jasmine shrieked as Esme lost her grip and the vase began to fall. In a split second Maddy acted, hurtling across the space between her and Esme, the room fading to a blur around her. As the vase toppled down to the floor, she sprang, her arms outstretched. She caught the vase just in time, landing beside Esme in perfect balance.

For a moment there was a stunned silence and then everyone began to talk at once. "Maddy!" Esme squealed. "How did you do that?"

"Oh my gosh, Maddy!"

"That was amazing!"

"So cool!"

Esme and her friends crowded round Maddy. Over their shoulders, Maddy saw Rachel. Hearing the noise, she had come hurrying towards them and was standing on the outskirts of the group, beaming and giving her a thumbs-up. Maddy knew that Rachel had guessed exactly how she'd done it!

"I still can't believe it," Esme went on. "I mean, you moved so fast, and the way you leaped into the air . . ." Her voice trailed off, her green eyes wide and impressed.

Maddy glowed. "It was nothing." She hid a smile, wondering what they'd all say if they knew the truth.

Suddenly she remembered Greykin, and her smile faded. She could feel his familiar cold weight in her pocket

– he must have climbed down there for safety, and turned ceramic again. Maddy touched his cool smoothness worriedly. If she'd already solved the problem, then he was going to have to leave again . . . but she'd hardly had any time with him at all!

"Well, thank you so, so much," said Esme fervently. "Here, I'll help you put it back on the stand." Maddy was one of the smallest in her class, and she couldn't even reach the top of the stand. Jasmine and Esme took the vase from her and put it back.

"Phew," Jasmine said, taking a deep breath when the vase was safely back in place. "Imagine if you'd broken it, Esme."

"I'd have been in *so* much trouble," Esme agreed. She wiped her forehead with a grin, pretending to shake sweat off her hand.

"Not just trouble," said Rachel, stepping forward.

Esme looked as surprised as if the mummy had spoken. "I'm sorry?"

Rachel stuck her hands on her hips. "It's a really valuable vase, part of history. It's thousands of years old! And you might have broken it, all because of some dumb dare."

Esme's eyebrows shot up. She glanced at her friends.

"At least everything worked out OK," said Maddy quickly, not wanting an argument. "I'm just glad I caught it."

"Yes, and in *such* a cool way," said Esme, forgetting Rachel and turning to her again. "You were like

Supergirl! Like, like this . . ." She imitated Maddy's leap and everyone laughed, apart from Rachel.

Esme smiled at Maddy. "Why don't you hang around with us for the rest of the day? We could do our questionnaires together." Seeing Maddy's clipboard on the floor, she picked it up. "You've already got loads of the answers. We could get the rest of them together – and do more dares on the way. What do you say?"

"I . . . er . . ." Maddy's cheeks flushed. Despite her worry over Greykin, a flicker of excitement ran through her. Esme, one of the most popular girls in their year, had actually asked her to join them! But what about Rachel? She glanced at her friend. Rachel looked cross and gave Maddy the tiniest shake of her head.

"What's the problem?" said Esme. "Come on. It'll be fun."

Maddy hesitated. "Rachel too?"

Esme didn't look thrilled, but she shrugged. "Sure. If she wants." She set off for the exit. "Come on, let's go to the next room."

"Maddy!" Rachel hissed, pulling her back from the others as they followed Esme. "What are you doing?

Why did you say we'd go around with *them*?"

"I . . . I just thought it might be fun." Maddy gave Rachel a hopeful look.

"As much fun as having a tooth taken out." Rachel huffed.

"Oh, don't be like that—" Maddy broke off as she felt Greykin come to life in her pocket. Ducking back into the empty Egyptian room, she pulled it open and the little cat stuck his head out, his fur ruffled. The two girls stopped quarrelling instantly.

"Greykin, we did it, we solved the problem," whispered Maddy. She bit her lip. She didn't want to say goodbye to him just yet! "But . . . this means you have to go, doesn't it?"

He shook his head as he climbed out onto her palm. "No, not just yet," he said, curling his tail around his legs. His eyes gleamed up at her. "You were wonderful, Maddy – well done for saving the vase. But my senses tell me that there's still more to come. I think we've only solved part of the problem."

"So you'll be staying for longer?" Maddy cried, hope fizzing through her.

Greykin nodded. "Until the whole problem has been solved."

"But what's the rest of the

problem?" asked Rachel in a hushed voice.

Greykin's eyes went to the door. "Esme," he said seriously. "I'm certain that it's still to do with her."

Just then Esme stuck her head back in. Instantly Greykin changed back to his ceramic form.

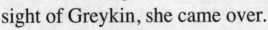

"Come on, Mads, what are you waiting for?" said Esme. Catching sight of Greykin, she came over. "What's that? Oh, it's a china cat – what a funny old thing! Why have you got it with you?" she laughed.

"Oh, he's just my . . . my lucky charm," Maddy invented, hastily putting Greykin away again.

Esme grinned. "You're seriously weird, Maddy. But I like you." She tucked her arm through Maddy's. "Come on! The others are waiting through there."

She started walking. Maddy shot a beseeching look over her shoulder at Rachel. Blowing out an unhappy breath, her friend followed them.

As they went around the museum, Esme stuck close to Maddy, including her in every conversation. Maddy would have been thrilled, but she was always uncomfortably aware of Rachel standing on the edge of the group, looking fed-up. *She could at least try to be friendly*, thought Maddy. Then she felt a twinge of

guilt. She knew that Rachel was
the friendliest person in the world,
normally.

Esme's interest in doing the
questionnaire soon waned, and instead
she started suggesting dares again.
In the Norman Conquest room, she
dared them all to walk along the back
of a row of armchair-like seats that
lined one wall. Rachel put her arms
over her chest. "No, thanks," she said
coolly.

"Suit yourself," laughed Esme.
"OK, we'll take turns guarding the
door. If anyone's coming, tell me!"

As Jasmine hovered by the open
doorway, keeping a lookout for
museum staff and other visitors, Esme
climbed up onto the first chair. She
managed to do it, teetering her way

across them. The other girls all fell off
when they tried, stifling their giggles.
Maddy's heart thudded when it was
her turn.

"Come on, Mads, I bet this'll be
easy for *you*," said Esme, nudging
her.

Maddy bit her lip, not able to look
at Rachel. She knew it was wrong, but

she couldn't refuse, not with Esme looking so expectantly at her. For a moment she was tempted to use her cat powers again, but she knew she couldn't: she was only supposed to use them in times of real need.

Swallowing hard, Maddy climbed up onto the first chair. Years of ballet had given her excellent balance, and

she made her way easily across the row, finally hopping nimbly to the ground. "See, I knew it!" said Esme, raising Maddy's hand up in the air like she was a champion. "Supergirl strikes again."

Maddy grinned, a warm glow flooding through her – though out of the corner of her eye she saw Rachel shake her head, looking disgusted. "I'm so glad today is almost over," she muttered to Maddy as they made their way back to the foyer where they were supposed to meet Mr Orwell. "Esme's driving me mad."

"Hey, Mads!" Esme called from behind them. "Come here a minute."

Maddy glanced at Rachel. Her friend rolled her eyes. "Go on, *Mads*," she said. "No doubt she'll have some other dumb dare for you to do."

"Rachel—" Maddy started. But her friend was already walking off.

Maddy stared after Rachel, feeling torn. Just then the others caught up. Esme ran a hand through her short hair, making it stick up in even cooler spikes. "Listen, I'm having a slumber party on Saturday night. Jaz, Sadie and Mia are all coming. Do you want to come too?"

The answer burst out of Maddy. "Oh, yes please!" she gasped. And then she realized something. "Rachel too?" she added uncertainly. She didn't really think her friend would want to go, but it would help if she was at least invited.

"Well, the thing is . . ." Esme shifted, looking awkward. "I can only invite four people, max. My mum will freak if I ask more. So really, it was just you I wanted to invite."

Maddy swallowed.

"What do you say?" Esme asked, smiling at her.

Maddy glanced around. Jasmine, Sadie and Mia, who had never seemed to notice her in the past, were looking at her eagerly, like they actually *wanted* her to join in and be there.

"OK. Thanks!" She could hardly say the words fast enough.

"Awesome!" Esme held her hand up in a high five and Maddy met it with a smile. As they went to the foyer, Maddy's thoughts were racing. A slumber party at Esme's would be amazing, but what would Rachel say? She bit her lip as she saw her waiting

with the rest of the class. She knew
that Rachel was going to be really
hurt when she found out.

But I've got to go, Maddy argued
guiltily to herself. There was still a
problem to do with Esme – if she
went to the slumber party, then she
might find out what it was. Surely
Rachel would understand that?

Chapter Three

Her best friend pulled a face as Maddy joined her. "So what did Esme want?" she asked in an undertone.

Maddy opened her mouth, and then closed it again. The thought of telling Rachel made her feel sick. No, she decided hastily. She'd explain later, when they were alone.

"Nothing much," she lied.

To her relief, just then Mr Orwell clapped his hands. "Quiet now, everyone. Let's do a head count." Maddy stared anxiously at the floor as Mr Orwell started counting. Though she knew she had to do it, she wasn't looking forward to telling Rachel the truth.

She wasn't looking forward to it at all.

Chapter Four

When Maddy told Greykin
about the slumber party that
afternoon, the little cat purred in
approval. "Perfect! It'll be just the
chance we need to watch Esme
closely and see what the problem is."
He was sitting on the desk near Nibs
and Ollie, his fur looking soft and
strokable compared to their ceramic
coolness.

Maddy nodded glumly.
Uncomfortable feelings swirled in her

stomach whenever she thought about
the sleepover, and the way she'd lied
to Rachel.

Greykin put his head on one side,
his whiskers twitching thoughtfully
as he regarded her. "Is something
wrong?"

"A bit," Maddy admitted, slumping
her chin onto her hand. "I – I'm just
worried about the slumber party."
At Greykin's puzzled look, she went
on, "You see, Rachel doesn't like
Esme. I mean, she *really* doesn't like
her."

Greykin nodded. "I see. She's not
looking forward to the party, then?"

"No, she hasn't been invited," said
Maddy.

Greykin blinked, looking confused.
Maddy felt surprise ripple through

her. He usually understood her so well that she hardly ever had to explain her feelings to him! "She'll be hurt that I'm going," she explained. "She's going to feel really left out."

"Ah," said Greykin, swishing his tail. Maddy could see that he still didn't really get it. After a pause, he said, "But if she doesn't like Esme, then surely she wouldn't want to go anyway? Never go where you're not wanted – that's certainly the way we cats would view it!"

Maddy sighed. If only it was that easy.

Padding over to her, Greykin gently rubbed his head against her finger. "Don't worry, Rachel's very sensible, for a human. She knows that the problem has to be solved – I'm sure she'll understand why you need to go."

"I hope so," said Maddy, trying to smile. But she knew perfectly well that Rachel wasn't going to understand at all . . . and that the longer she put off telling her, the worse it was going to be.

Greykin suddenly jumped down from the desk. Landing neatly on her

knees, he bounded to the floor. "I think it's time for a game," he said with a merry look in his eyes. "How about hide and seek?"

Maddy sighed. "Greykin, I don't really feel like— oh!" she broke off as he pounced playfully on her foot and then darted away again.

"Start counting now!" he called over his shoulder.

Maddy hesitated, and then let her worries slip away. *I'll tell Rachel tomorrow*, she promised herself. For now, she had Greykin with her once more – and she was going to enjoy every second of it.

"All right – but I bet I can find you!" she said with a grin. And closing her eyes, she started to count.

* * *

But as the next day passed, somehow Maddy couldn't find the right moment to talk to Rachel. Each time she tried, the words just dried up inside her. Finally, during afternoon break, she decided that she simply *had* to tell her, and pulled her over to one side in the playground.

"Um, Rachel . . ." she said hesitantly.

But her friend was hardly listening – she was full of news about the science club, which Mrs Pratt had asked her to help organize. "It's going to be brilliant!" she said, her eyes shining behind her glasses. "We're going to make all sorts of amazing things. Mrs Pratt and I are looking up some experiments on the internet, and we're going to try them out this week.

You are going to join when it starts,
aren't you?"

Maddy wasn't that interested in
science, but the last thing she wanted
was another reason to fall out with
Rachel. "Sure," she said. She took
a deep breath. "But Rachel, listen –
about Esme . . ."

Grimacing, Rachel glanced across
the playground to where Esme and the
others were messing about. "Oh, let's
not talk about Esme, Maddy! I know
we have to spend time with her so you
can find out what the problem is, but
she's so annoying."

"She isn't!" Maddy protested.
"She's really fun, and—"

"And always doing stupid things!"
interrupted Rachel. "She's going to
get into real trouble with all the dares

she's doing if she carries on."

Feeling torn, Maddy didn't reply.

Rachel squeezed her arm. "Come on, let's forget about Esme for now. How's Greykin?"

Maddy hesitated. She knew that she should tell Rachel about the slumber party, but she hated the thought of upsetting her. "He's fine," she said

finally. "We played hide and seek last night, and I won! He was hiding in the middle of my cuddly toys – I caught him when he blinked."

Rachel grinned. "You know, I've been thinking that we could improve his ladder," she said, referring to the cardboard ladder that Greykin used to climb up and down from Maddy's chest of drawers. "My dad has some wooden rods that he uses for gardening – one of those would make a brilliant ladder for him. Why don't I measure the distance next time I come, so I can get him one?"

"Oh, yes!" cried Maddy, imagining Greykin on a proper wooden ladder. She loved watching the little cat prowl up and down as he climbed, and she knew that Rachel did too. "Why don't

you come round tomorrow, after
school?"

As the two friends talked and
planned, Maddy tried to tell herself
that everything was going to be OK.
Maybe Greykin was right, and Rachel
wouldn't mind about the slumber
party when she found out, after all.

Oh, please let that be true, thought
Maddy fervently. *Please!*

"All right, everyone, it's time to hand
your papers in," called Mr Orwell. It
was the next morning, during maths.
Writing her name neatly on her
worksheet, Maddy passed it along
with the others.

From outside came the sound of
an engine. Glancing out the window,
Maddy saw the school lunch van

pulling out of the drive, leaving at its usual time.

"You know what would be great?" she heard Esme whisper to Jasmine. "If we could sneak outside somehow and get in the van, and then *vroom*! Off we'd go, and we'd get to miss maths! Mr Orwell would never find us." Esme and the others giggled. Maddy looked down, stifling a smile. Beside her, Rachel rolled her eyes.

The morning dragged on. Finally, it was almost time for break. "Listen up, everyone!" Mr Orwell clapped his hands. "The other teachers and

I are getting some lunchtime clubs
sorted out. Make sure you sign up in
the hall if you're interested in joining.
There's going to be science club" –
Rachel nudged Maddy and grinned
– "art club, computer club and sports
club – we'll be playing basketball
and football this term," Mr Orwell
continued.

"Are you going to join the sports
club?" Maddy heard Jasmine ask
Esme.

"No way. Boooring!" Esme
replied.

"I'll be running the sports club, so
who might join?" Quite a few of the
class put their hands up. Mr Orwell
smiled. "Great! Esme, how about
you?" he asked, catching sight of
Esme whispering to Jasmine.

Maddy saw Esme jump.
"No, um – I'm not
interested in
sports." She
blushed.

Maddy
stared at her
in surprise. It
wasn't like
Esme to look so
uncomfortable.
But just then
the bell rang for
break, and she forgot about it.

"All right, off you go," called
Mr Orwell.

"Come on!" Esme said. Jumping to
her feet, she led the way outside.

Rachel pulled Maddy back. "Can't
we do something on our own again

this break?" she appealed. "It was so nice yesterday when it was just the two of us, talking."

Maddy wavered. It *had* been nice . . . but at the same time, she really wanted to be with Esme and the others. "I should probably stay with Esme," she said awkwardly. "You know Greykin told me I need to stay close to her." The little cat was in her pocket that day, curled up in his ceramic form. Maddy touched him, feeling comforted just by having him there.

Looking reluctant, Rachel followed her outside. They walked down the side of the building to the main playground, where Esme and the others were sitting on a wall.

"Hey, Mads!" Esme called. She

shifted along and made a space beside her. "Come and sit by me. So, what are we going to do today?" she said, looking around at them all. "What should the dare be?"

The girls looked at each other. "We don't always have to do dares," Sadie said cautiously.

Esme blinked. "Not do dares?"

"We could play something else," Jasmine suggested.

Hope rushed up inside of Maddy. If Esme could be persuaded to do something else, maybe Rachel would join in, instead of standing on the edge looking so stiff and fed-up.

Esme raised her eyebrows. "Hmm, let me see. What other cool games could we play?" She put her head on one side as if she was thinking hard.

"Ooh, I know! Let's play something with magic in it!"

Maddy opened her mouth to eagerly agree when Esme burst out laughing. "And how dumb would that be?" she hooted. "As if any of us would be babyish enough to actually care about magic, right, Maddy?" she said, nudging her.

Maddy forced a smile. She didn't dare meet Rachel's eyes. Guiltily touching her pocket, she felt relieved that Greykin was still in his ceramic form and hadn't heard.

"No, it's got to be dares," Esme declared. "'Cos I've just thought of a *really* good one. I dare one of you to climb up the drainpipe and get that ball out of the gutter."

Everyone looked at where Esme was pointing. Maddy's eyes went up and up. In the gutter, just under the school roof, lay a small red ball that was stuck.

"That looks really hard!" protested Sadie.

Jasmine shook her head. "Yeah, it's too high up, Esme."

"But *Maddy* could do it!" burst out Mia suddenly. "Remember the way she climbed the drainpipe last year, everyone?"

Maddy swallowed. That had been when she'd had to rescue Sherry Newton, the school bully, with her cat powers – which had then abandoned her halfway through!

"*Really?*" Esme's face lit up. She clutched Maddy's arm. "Oh, well this is *your* dare, then. Definitely!"

Maddy's mouth went dry. Before she could say anything, Rachel jumped in. "Don't be stupid, Esme," she snapped. "Of course she's not doing it – it's way too dangerous."

Irritation swept over Maddy. Rachel sounded like her mum! From Esme's laughing eyes, she knew that she was thinking the same thing. "Maddy's not scared, are you, Maddy?" said Esme.

Maddy hesitated for only a moment.

She'd got into trouble for climbing the drainpipe last time, but at least she knew she could do it, even without her cat powers. "No, I'm not scared," she said, trying to sound cool and confident. "It's easy-peasy."

"*What?*" spluttered Rachel. "But Maddy—"

"You'll really try it, Mads?" said Esme eagerly.

Maddy nodded, and jumped down from the wall.

"Go, Maddy!" Esme started a chant. "Go, Maddy! Go, Maddy!" The others – apart from Rachel – joined in too.

Suddenly Maddy wished she hadn't agreed to this. She couldn't back down now, though. Esme would think she was a total coward. Quickly, she checked to see where the teacher on duty was, but she was busy dealing with a boy from Reception who had fallen over, leading him inside to get a plaster.

Taking a deep breath, Maddy went over and stood at the bottom of the drainpipe. Suddenly she felt a tingling on her cheeks, and her spirits fell. Oh no, not now! She glanced back at Esme and the others. She *couldn't* refuse to do the dare – she just couldn't.

Ignoring the tingling, Maddy started to climb, grabbing the drainpipe with both hands and then pulling herself up, gripping with her legs. She could feel everyone watching. To her relief, it really *wasn't* very hard, so long as she didn't look down. In

a few moments she'd reached the top. Stretching, she grabbed the ball and threw it free, and then shimmied quickly down again. She blew out a breath when her feet touched the ground. *Done it!*

To her relief, the tingling feeling seemed to have vanished. Turning, Maddy couldn't hold back a grin at the impressed look on Esme's face. She jogged back over to the wall. A few people were pointing at her, but most of the other children were caught up in their own games and hadn't noticed.

"Brilliant!" Esme cried as Maddy reached them. She drummed her heels excitedly on the wall. "Wow, you really *can* climb."

"See, I told you," said Mia proudly.

Double Dare

Jasmine and Sadie crowded around, congratulating her. The only person not to join in was Rachel. She was hanging back, a frown on her face. Suddenly Maddy felt guilty – and then cross that she felt guilty! She knew that she shouldn't have taken the dare, but did Rachel have to look so disapproving?

"You really are the champion dare-doer, Maddy Lloyd." Esme was

saying, her eyes shining. "And as a prize, you can choose where you want to sleep at my slumber party on Saturday. There are bunk beds and three camp beds, and *you* can have first choice!"

Maddy gulped. Biting her lip, she looked slowly across at Rachel.

Her friend's mouth had fallen open. She was staring at Maddy with a look of hurt incredulity on her face. Maddy didn't know what to say or do. Rachel stared for a moment longer, and then she turned and marched off.

Chapter Five

Maddy felt as if she'd just had a bucket of ice cubes dumped over her. She'd never meant for Rachel to find out about the slumber party like this! Now what was she going to do?

"Um – I'll be right back," she muttered. Before Esme or the others could react, she dashed after Rachel, catching up with her halfway across the playground. She tugged on her arm. "Rachel, wait—"

Her friend turned on her. "I can't believe you're going to Esme's for a slumber party – *and you didn't tell me*!"

Maddy faltered. "Well, I was going to . . . I mean . . ."

Rachel glared at her, tapping her foot. "When did she ask you?" she demanded.

Maddy bit her lip. "At . . . at the museum," she admitted.

"That was the day before yesterday, Maddy! You mean you've known all this time and you haven't said anything?"

Maddy tried a different tack. "Rachel, I *have* to go to the party. Greykin—"

"Oh, don't even say it." Rachel interrupted angrily. "It's *not* because of Greykin and the problem that you're going. You just *want* to go to Esme's slumber party, and you don't even care if I'm invited or not."

"That's not true!"

"It *is*, Maddy! You're like a different person when you're with Esme. Doing dumb dares all the time, and agreeing with her that magic is babyish."

"I *didn't* agree with her!" said Maddy hotly. "I just . . ." she trailed off guiltily, remembering her silence. In her pocket, she could feel the small, still weight of Greykin in his ceramic form.

"You just didn't tell her what you really think," finished Rachel.

Maddy felt her cheeks turn pink. "Look, you know that I've got to try and be friends with her—"

"Well, go and be friends with her then," snapped Rachel. "That's just fine by me." She stalked away.

"Rachel!"

But Rachel didn't look round. Maddy felt close to tears. She *had* to spend time with Esme; how else was she meant to solve the problem? But actually, Rachel was right, a small voice inside her admitted. It wasn't just that she had to hang around with Esme – she *liked* it. It was a lot of fun to be part of the popular crowd for a change.

Maddy jumped as a set of sharp claws dug into her leg through her trouser pocket. Greykin! She hurried to the girls' toilets in the cloakroom. Luckily there was no one else in there. Locking herself in a cubicle, she took the little cat out of her pocket.

"Well?" he demanded from her palm.

"Well, what?" Maddy whispered back – and then with a sinking heart, she remembered the tickling feeling that had swept her cheeks just as she started to climb.

Greykin was staring at her incredulously, his golden eyes round.

"Well, what?" he repeated. "Maddy, didn't you feel your whiskers tingling?"

She swallowed hard, not wanting to admit that she had felt the tingling, but then ignored it. "Sort of," she said weakly.

"*Sort of?*" Greykin echoed, flexing his tiny claws. "But the signals were there, loud and clear!" he huffed. "Well, at least now we know what the

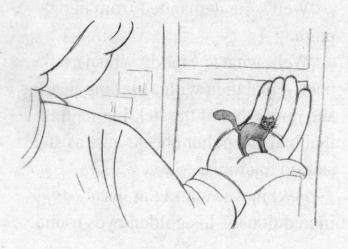

problem is." Sitting down on her hand
he gave her a cool look as she gaped
at him. "If you keep your mouth open
like that, a fly will go in." . .

Maddy shut her mouth with a snap.
"So . . . what *is* the problem?" she
asked finally.

Greykin began washing himself,
rubbing his paw over his face,
taking his time. Maddy bit back her
impatience. "Greykin, please. I'm
really sorry I didn't do anything about
my whiskers tingling. Will you tell me
what the problem is?"

The tiny cat looked up and regarded
Maddy gravely. "The problem is
Esme's dares – they're getting out
of hand and someone is going to get
seriously hurt. We have to put a stop
to them!"

* * *

Maddy hardly said a thing for the rest of that afternoon. Greykin's words kept beating through her mind. What was she going to do? She could just imagine how Esme would laugh if she, Maddy, told her she had to stop doing dares. She'd probably decide she didn't want Maddy to be in their group any more. Maddy's stomach twisted at the thought.

She wished she could talk to Rachel, but her best friend was still in a mood with her. When school ended, Rachel hurried into the cloakroom and grabbed her coat.

"Rachel! Wait!" Maddy ran after her. "Aren't you coming back to mine?"

Rachel shook her head, not meeting

Maddy's eyes. "No, I'm going home.
Why don't you ask Esme instead?"
And turning, she walked away.

Maddy headed slowly home, hardly
listening to Jack as he chatted to her
all the way. As soon as they got in,
she went up to her room and shut
the door. Taking Greykin out of her
pocket, she sat on her bed and stroked
his soft back. "Oh, Greykin, what am

I going to do?" she sighed.

He stared at her in surprise from her palm. "You know what you have to do. You have to stop the dares."

Maddy swallowed. "But – if I try to stop the dares, Esme and the others might not want to be my friend any more."

Greykin rubbed his soft head against her fingers. "Maddy, the magic is very important," he reminded her gently. "You can't just ignore it. There must be a very real danger of something bad happening, or else I wouldn't be here. We have to stop it."

Maddy nodded slowly. He was right, but she didn't like it. If Esme fell out with her, she'd be back to being Maddy Nobody at school – and if Rachel carried on not talking to her,

she wouldn't have any friends left at
all.

"So we must decide what to do,"
continued Greykin, curling his tail
around her thumb. "We must plan our
attack!"

Chewing her lip, Maddy burst out,
"Well – I could always wait until after
the slumber party. I mean . . . while
I'm there, I might see something
happening, or come up with an idea."

Greykin frowned. Leaping from
her palm, he hopped onto Maddy's
bedside table, where he perched
beside her ballerina lamp. "But the
slumber party is on Saturday – that's
three days away! We shouldn't wait
that long."

Maddy's heart pounded. She knew
they shouldn't hesitate now that they

knew what the problem was, but
she couldn't bear the thought of not
going to the slumber party on top of
everything else. "It'll be fine," she
assured him. "I'll keep a really close
eye on Esme in school this week, in
case anything happens. But I'm sure
I'll be able to think of a plan more
easily after the party."

She held her breath. From the
bedside table, Greykin stared at her
with his shrewd golden eyes, not

answering. Suddenly she had the feeling that he knew exactly what was going on in her head. It was bad enough arguing with Rachel – now it seemed like Greykin was disappointed in her too.

Feeling uncomfortable, Maddy got to her feet. "I . . . I might just go and see if Mum needs help getting tea ready. I'll see you later, Greykin." And with cheeks flushing red, she hurried out of the room.

Maddy's week didn't improve. Rachel continued not speaking to her, spending the breaks reading on her own or planning the science club with Mrs Pratt. Maddy really missed her. She played dares with Esme and the others, but she couldn't enjoy it. Every time Esme suggested something, Maddy tensed, worrying that maybe something was going to go seriously wrong, and knowing that sooner or later she was going to spoil everyone's fun by stopping the dares.

She wasn't even enjoying having Greykin at home. He clearly disapproved of her decision to leave trying to stop Esme's dares until after the slumber party, and spent much of his time in his ceramic form. Maddy sat at her desk, staring glumly at his cold, painted face. Usually she and Greykin were so close! He always went everywhere with her, tucked in her pocket, and they talked about anything and everything. Now it was as if he hadn't come to life at all.

Sadness ached through Maddy.

She reached out, starting to touch Greykin with her finger, and then she stopped. Though she knew the current awkwardness between them was mostly her own fault, it wasn't *all* her fault . . . He really could be a bit more understanding. He was usually so kind and wise!

Maddy grimaced, fighting tears as hurt and anger swept over her. She wanted things with Greykin to be like they always were – but why should *she* be the one to back down? It was like he wasn't even trying to imagine how she might be feeling!

Never mind, she thought, shoving her chair back and getting up from her desk. Let Greykin be cross with her, if he wanted. At least she had the slumber party to look forward to. A smile tugged at her lips at the thought.

Every time Maddy thought of the party, a rush of excitement fizzed through her. Esme talked practically non-stop about all the cool things that they'd be doing. And best of all was the fact that she, Maddy Lloyd, was one of the very few people Esme had invited. At school, it was as if she and the other girls had an invisible glow around them. For once in her life, she was someone who other people in her class wanted to be! And she was going to enjoy it – no matter what Greykin and Rachel thought.

When Saturday afternoon came, Maddy packed her things eagerly, hardly able to believe that the big day had finally arrived. Folding her pyjamas, she tucked them into her bag along with her clothes for the next day, toothbrush, toothpaste and hairbrush.

"Maddy! It's time to go," her mum shouted up the stairs.

"Coming!" Maddy zipped up her case and went to her desk to pick up Greykin. He was in his ceramic form, sitting bolt upright. His usually friendly face looked serious, just as it had for days now.

Maddy hesitated. She knew that Greykin expected her to take him to the party with her, but what if Esme suggested a dare and Greykin insisted she had to stop it? That would be awful. Maddy stepped back, biting her lip.

"Maddy! Come on!"

Suddenly deciding, Maddy grabbed her case. She wasn't going to take Greykin after all. She was going to have fun at the party – and then, once it was over, she'd somehow put a stop to the dares.

Trying not to look at the little cat's disapproving face, Maddy ran out of the room, her heart pounding.

Chapter Six

Maddy watched the houses rush by from the car window. Panic clawed inside her. How was Greykin going to feel when he realized that she'd left him behind? She cringed at the thought. "Mum!" she said quickly. "Can we go back? I've forgotten something."

"Oh, I'm sorry, sweetie," her mum said. "But we haven't got time. I have to collect Jack from his karate lesson after dropping you off. Is it something really important?"

Maddy swallowed hard. "It's . . . it's Greykin. I should have brought him."

Her mum gave her a sympathetic look. "Oh, darling, never mind. He'll probably be safer at home, and you'll be too busy with the others to have time to play with him. Did you say there are going to be five of you altogether?"

Maddy nodded.

"Goodness!" Mrs Lloyd blinked. "Esme's mum is a lot braver than me!"

She drove on. Maddy felt close to tears. What if Greykin was really cross with her? Suddenly all she wanted was to be going home to see him. She didn't want to be going to the slumber party at all.

They pulled up outside Esme's
house – a large modern home on the
new housing estate. As Maddy got
out of the car with her mum, the front
door was pulled open.

"Mads!" Esme squealed. She was
looking very cool in a miniskirt with
ripped tights and a crop top. She had
spiked up her hair even more than
usual and put pink dye on the ends.
Jasmine and Sadie were with her,

dressed as if they were going out:
Jasmine in skinny gold jeans and a
matching T-shirt, and Sadie in a short
flippy skirt and leggings. Maddy
suddenly felt quite babyish in her
usual blue jeans and lilac T-shirt.

Sadie had a bag of make-up in
her hands. "We're going to do
makeovers!"

"And do our hair!" cried Jasmine,

waving a pair of straighteners.

"And dance!" cried Esme.

Maddy's mum looked slightly stunned. "OK – well, great. Is your mum around, Esme?"

Esme disappeared inside and reappeared with her mum. "Let's leave them to talk," she said, picking up Maddy's case and taking it inside. Music was blaring out. Esme dragged

Maddy through to the lounge. There were crisps and biscuits on the table, more make-up, nail varnish, hair spray.

"Let's get started," Esme said, sitting down. "Mia said she's going to be a bit late. Jaz, you and Sadie can make me up and then when we've all had makeovers we can dance!"

Jasmine and Sadie set to work with the make-up and nail varnish.

"I'll . . . I'll just say goodbye to my mum," Maddy said, feeling a bit out of her depth. She went to the door. Her mum was still talking to Mrs Dawson. "I'm just off now," she said to Maddy. "Have a lovely time."

"Thanks." Maddy desperately wanted to hug her but didn't want any of the others to see in case they teased her. She felt the start of tears prickle in her eyes and blinked them back hastily. "See you tomorrow."

She waved her mum off and Mrs Dawson shut the door. She smiled at Maddy. "Can I get you a drink?"

"Yes please." Maddy didn't really want to go back to join the others just yet and she gratefully followed Mrs Dawson into the large kitchen. She could hear their giggles and squeals from the lounge above the music. Maddy really wished Rachel was here. Suddenly Esme and the others just seemed so different to her – and she was going to be spending a whole night with them.

Mrs Dawson seemed really nice, though. She was wearing a tracksuit and had her hair tied back in a loose ponytail. It was funny, Maddy thought. She'd have expected Esme to have a mum who was really into fashion and make-up.

Mrs Dawson fetched a glass. "I'm so glad Esme's made friends with you all so quickly," she told Maddy. "She was quite worried about it when she moved schools."

Maddy stared. She couldn't imagine Esme being worried about making friends! She saw some photos of Esme in frames on the sideboard  and went to look at them.

In the photos, Esme looked very different. Her short hair hadn't been spiked up and she wasn't wearing any make-up. In fact, she looked almost like a boy! There were photos of her in  different sports kits, holding trophies and smiling at the camera.

Mrs Dawson brought the juice over.

"Thank you," said Maddy gratefully. "What did Esme win all those trophies for?"

"All the different sports she plays – well, used to play before we moved here," Mrs Dawson gave the photos a proud look. "Esme's won trophies for tennis and netball, swimming and running. I keep meaning to look into some outside-school clubs, but I haven't had a chance yet. It's such a pity your school doesn't have a sports club. I think Esme really misses it."

Maddy frowned. "But we . . ."

Just then the door opened and Esme burst in. She had glittering silver eyeshadow and dark mascara on, lipgloss and a lilac shimmer on her cheeks. "There you are, Mads! What are you doing in here? It's your turn for a makeover."

"See you later, Maddy!" Mrs Dawson smiled.

Maddy let herself be dragged away, her thoughts bouncing around in her head. Why had Esme told her mum there was no sports club at school? And why hadn't she signed up for anything if she liked sports so much? Maddy remembered how Esme

had just laughed and said sport was 'boring'.

Esme pulled her over to the chair. "Maddy's turn!" she cried, and before Maddy knew it, she didn't have time to think about it any more as Jasmine approached her, brandishing an eyeshadow brush.

Maddy had never been to a slumber party like it. Esme's energy never seemed to wane, and she bounced from one thing to another. When they were all made up, they went outside and she got her two skateboards out. Esme turned out to be brilliant at skateboarding, and tried to teach them all to do tricks. But none of them could manage it. Maddy knew her cat powers wouldn't help, even if she could use them – somehow she had a feeling that cats weren't very good on skateboards!

Double Dare

After skateboarding, Esme gave
them each a slumber party present
of a set of multi-coloured bracelets,
just like her own, and then they had
a dancing competition. Maddy loved
dancing – particularly ballet – but
she just didn't feel in the mood that
day. She felt strange wearing so much
make-up and it almost felt like an
effort to have to smile all the time
and join in. To think this was the
sleepover she'd been looking forward
to so much!

A pang went through her as she
thought of Rachel, sitting on her own
at home. And had Greykin realized
that Maddy had left without him yet?
She winced, and wished with all her
heart that he was here. Just to have his
familiar warm weight in her pocket

would have made her feel much better.

When they'd finished dancing, Esme dragged the sofa cushions on to the floor. "Sit down, everyone!"

They all collapsed, pink in the face from dancing. Sadie flopped backwards. "I'm exhausted."

"Me too," said Mia.

"Let's think of something else to do!" said Esme eagerly.

"Something that involves sitting down," said Sadie, fanning herself.

"OK." Esme thought for a moment. "How about we plan some dares for school? We should have a competition – see who can think of the most daring thing! You can all think of them, and I'll be the judge."

Maddy caught her breath as her

cheeks started to tingle. Suddenly
she had a very bad feeling about this!
Esme turned to her. "You're good at
dares, Mads. What can you think up?"

"Um," Maddy stammered. "I . . . I
don't know. Maybe setting off a stink
bomb again?" That might be smelly,
but at least it wasn't dangerous.

Esme didn't look impressed. "Boring! I've already done that. Who can think of something better?"

"Write something about Mr Orwell on the whiteboard?" Mia suggested.

Esme looked about as impressed with that idea as she had been with the stink bomb. "Hmm," she said.

"I know!" exclaimed Jasmine, bouncing on her knees. "What about setting the school fire alarm off?"

Esme grinned. "Now we're talking! Nice one, Jaz."

Uneasiness shivered through Maddy. They could really get into trouble if they were caught.

"Ooh, I've got one too!" said Sadie, and all at once Maddy's cheeks were prickling even more. "You know how we're not allowed skateboards at school?" They all nodded. "Well, how about you sneak your skateboard into school and go round the playground on it at break time, Esme?"

Esme's green eyes started gleaming. "Or even better . . . how about I take my skateboard in and then when the school lunch van leaves, I'll hold on to the back and hitch a ride through the car park!"

They all gaped. Maddy hands flew to her face – her cheeks felt like they were on fire. "That's way too dangerous!" she exclaimed. "You can't do that!"

Esme's expression grew stubborn. "Says who?"

Maddy gulped. She really didn't want Esme getting cross with her, but she couldn't let her do a dare like that.

"Please . . . please don't," she begged.

Esme turned her back on her. "I'm going to do it!" she declared. "So, Sadie wins the competition for best dare."

Maddy fell silent, biting her lip. She desperately wanted to say something more, to argue. But how could she?

Double Dare

Esme would just get cross with her, and all the others probably would too.

"When are you going to do it?" Jasmine asked eagerly.

"Monday!" Esme ran her hand through her hair, looking smug.

"But how?" Mia's eyes were wide. "The lunch van comes while we're sitting in class."

"Hmm, yes, I'll need a distraction . . . something that will get me out of the classroom long enough to do it." Esme tapped her finger against her teeth for a moment. "Ha! I have it!"

"What?" said Maddy nervously.

Esme shook her head. "I'm not telling – you'll see! It'll be almost as good as the dare itself, I promise."

"You're a nutter," said Sadie with a grin.

"That's me!" Esme jumped to her feet. "Let's go and get some food. We've got pizza for tea."

The others all scrambled to their feet and went into the kitchen, talking and laughing. Maddy stood up very slowly. Worry churned through her as she thought about Monday.

Somehow, she had to stop Esme from doing such a dangerous dare – but how?

Chapter Seven

"So how was it?" asked Maddy's mum as they drove away the next day.

"Fine," Maddy muttered, slumping back in the car seat.

Her mum looked at her. "Only fine?"

Maddy managed a smile. "No, it . . . it was good." It wasn't a complete lie. After supper, Esme had calmed down a bit and they'd all played Cluedo, one of Maddy's favourite board games, and then

they'd watched a DVD. Afterwards,
in bed, Esme had told them all ghost
stories. If Maddy hadn't been so
worried about the dare on Monday –
and missing Greykin and Rachel – she
would have enjoyed herself.

"You didn't tell me that Rachel
hadn't been invited, Maddy," her
mum said.

Maddy chewed a fingernail. "Esme
could only ask four people."

"Did Rachel mind?"

"A bit," Maddy admitted.

"Oh." Her mum looked at her, her
eyes concerned, but she didn't say
anything more.

An idea jumped into Maddy's head.
"Mum, could we stop at Rachel's
house on the way home? I'd really
like to see her."

Her mum smiled. "Of course we can, sweetie. I haven't seen Rachel's mum since school started. We can have a coffee and you girls can play for a while."

Maddy felt relieved. The slumber party had made her realize just how much she missed Rachel. Esme and the others were fun, but whenever she was with them she felt like she was pretending a bit. It was never like that with Rachel.

She licked her suddenly dry lips. She just hoped that Rachel would want to be friends again.

When they knocked on the door, Rachel opened it. Behind her glasses, her blue eyes widened. Suddenly Maddy was very glad that her mum was standing beside her.

Chapter Seven

"Hi, Rachel," said Mrs Lloyd cheerfully. "We were just passing and thought we'd call in. Is your mum around?"

"Um . . . yes, she's in the kitchen."

"Great, I'll go on through. Why don't you two girls run and play for a while?"

Rachel looked reluctant, but she couldn't do much about it. "Sure," she muttered briefly. Not saying another word, she turned and walked up the stairs to her room. Maddy followed, her heart beating loudly.

They reached Rachel's room. Rachel went to her desk, keeping her back to Maddy. They stood in silence for a moment.

"So, how was the slumber party?" Rachel's voice was tight.

Maddy stared at Rachel's bristling back. "Oh, Rachel, I'm sorry!" she burst out. She ran over and put a hand on her friend's arm. "I shouldn't have gone to it when Esme didn't invite you. It was really stupid of me."

Rachel looked at her.

"Can we be friends again – please?"

To her delight, Rachel's face broke into a grin. "Of course we can, you doofus!" She hugged her. "Oh, Maddy, I've missed you so much. It was horrible seeing you with the others and just being on my own."

"I've missed you too," Maddy told her, happiness racing through her. "And I've got so much to tell you!"

"About the cats?" Rachel pulled back, her expression eager.

Maddy nodded. "Greykin and I know what the problem is, but" – she shook her head – "I've got absolutely no idea what to do about it."

Double Dare

Rachel's eyes gleamed. "OK, sit down and let's talk!"

They sat on her bed and Maddy told Rachel everything. "You were so right about Esme and her dares," she finished up miserably. "I should have listened. What am I going to do? How am I going to stop her?"

Looking deep in thought, Rachel adjusted her glasses. "It's difficult," she agreed. "But we'll think of something."

Maddy glowed at the word 'we'. "I know, why don't we ask if you can come back to mine now, and we can talk about it with Greykin? You've not really had a chance to see him properly yet. Though he probably isn't talking to me right now," she added, feeling worried again. She

knew she had some more making up
to do!

Maddy and Rachel's mums agreed
that Rachel could go to Maddy's for
lunch, and soon the two girls were
entering Maddy's bedroom. Maddy's
gaze went straight to her desk, where
Greykin was sitting in his ceramic form.

"Greykin?" she said softly, sliding
into the desk chair.

At first there was no response . . .
and then, slowly, the little cat
shimmered into life. He stared coldly
at her, the tip of his tail twitching.
"Well?" he said.

Maddy winced. "Oh, Greykin, I'm
sorry!" she cried. "I know I shouldn't
have gone to the party without you.
Please don't be upset – I tried to
get Mum to come back for you, but

she wouldn't."

"Hmm," said Greykin, his expression softening slightly.

"Maddy really is sorry, Greykin,"

Rachel put in, leaning towards him.
"Don't be cross; we all need to work
together. Something awful's going to
happen!"

The tiny cat's eyes widened in
alarm. "What?" he demanded.

Quickly, Maddy
explained, her words
tumbling over each
other. To her relief,
when she'd finished
Greykin nudged his
tiny nose against her
finger. "Good work,
Maddy. You've done very well to
discover what we need to do. We
must stop this dare!"

Relief surged through Maddy –
Greykin seemed to have forgiven
her. "But how?" she asked, stroking

his back. "Esme's *so* set on doing it –
she'll just laugh at me if I tell her not
to."

"Maybe we could tell Mr Orwell
about Esme bringing her skateboard
in," Rachel suggested.

Maddy shook her head. "Too easy,"
she said. She knew the way the
cat magic worked. If there was an
easy solution then it wasn't the right
one!

Greykin paced up and down the
desk. "This whole matter requires
careful consideration," he mused.
"Stopping this dare on its own isn't
going to be enough. The problem's
bigger than that – I believe we're
supposed to stop Esme from ever
doing dares again."

Maddy felt her scalp grow cold.

How was she supposed to do *that*?

"But that's going to be impossible!" protested Rachel.

Greykin sat on his haunches, golden eyes narrowed in thought. "It does seem very tricky . . . but never say never. For the moment, we simply need to concentrate on keeping Esme safe from harm. So, she'll be bringing her skateboard into school tomorrow?"

Maddy and Rachel nodded.

"Then you need to steal it," Greykin said matter-of-factly. He saw their shocked faces. "Only temporarily," he assured them. "Just so Esme can't do anything dangerous with it."

"But how am I supposed to steal it?" Maddy said anxiously.

Rachel groaned. "Oh, if only Nibs

was here you could make yourself shadowy!" The cat power that Nibs gave to Maddy was the ability to turn herself almost invisible. It had been invaluable at times.

Greykin cleared his throat sharply, his claws popping out for a brief moment. "Well, unfortunately Nibs is not here. However, even without her, I do not think all hope is lost. Maddy, there are still elements to your cat-prowess that you haven't explored yet."

"*Really*?" said Maddy, propping her forearms on the desk.

"Really. So even though I cannot give you the ability to turn invisible – like Nibs," he said with a slightly frosty look at Rachel, "you can still use cat stealth."

"Cat stealth," breathed Maddy. It sounded amazing!

"It will let you slip in and out of places without being noticed," explained Greykin. "You'll have to concentrate hard to make the magic work, but you should be able to steal the skateboard."

Rachel squeezed her hand. "And I'll distract Esme and keep her out of the way, just to make extra sure! We can do it at break time."

"But how will you keep her out of the way?" asked Maddy. "You know what she's like – she doesn't do anything she doesn't want to."

"I'll think of something," Rachel assured her. "Don't worry, it'll be fine. I promise!"

Seeing the determined set of Rachel's chin, Maddy felt her worries fade. If anyone could solve a problem once she put her mind to it, it was Rachel! "Thanks," she said with a smile. She was so glad that she and Rachel were friends again.

"Now then, your new power is very simple," said Greykin. "Maddy, all you have to do is think *cat stealth*. Then when you feel the magic begin, concentrate as hard as you can – and off you go!"

"OK," said Maddy eagerly, jumping up from the chair. "Shall I try it now?"

Greykin nodded, and Maddy closed her eyes. *Cat stealth*, she thought. *Cat stealth!* In seconds, the familiar electric sensation was sweeping through her. It grew stronger and stronger. Maddy opened her eyes, feeling almost dizzy.

Rachel peered at her. "How do you feel? You look just the same."

"I don't feel the same," managed Maddy. The magic felt like a tense rubber band inside of her, ready to go off with a *zing*!

Greykin hopped up onto her
stapler, his tail swishing eagerly.
"Try going for a prowl
downstairs, and see if anyone
notices you."

Maddy was
away almost
before he'd
finished talking,
slipping out of
her room and
then down the

stairs. This was amazing! She wasn't
making a sound; it was as if her feet
were barely touching the floor. And
although she wasn't shadowy, it was
like she had a cloak that said *don't
notice me* wrapped around her.

Buzzing with the magic, Maddy
went into the kitchen, where Jack

was just taking a carton of juice out
of the fridge. He didn't even look up
as she stealthily circled the room and
then slipped out again. Holding back a
grin, Maddy crept into the study next,
standing unseen at her father's elbow
as he typed at the computer. This
was so cool! He didn't know she was
there.

Suddenly her father's arm moved back as he clicked the mouse, knocking against Maddy. They both jumped.

"Where did *you* come from?" he asked, staring at her in confusion. "I didn't hear you come in."

"Nowhere," said Maddy hastily. The cat magic was gone now, leaving her standing there like a numpty! She backed out of the room, stifling a giggle. "I just, um – wanted to say hi!"

Maddy spent the rest of the afternoon practising, until finally she, Rachel and Greykin were convinced that she had got the hang of the magic. "Well done," purred Greykin, sitting back on his haunches.

Rachel nodded. "It really is

amazing, Maddy – I can hardly even see you when you're skulking about. I mean, I *can*, but . . ." she trailed off, looking perplexed.

"Cat stealth," said Greykin proudly. "We cats do not draw attention to ourselves when we don't want to!" He cleared his throat, wrapping his tail neatly around his legs. "And now that that's sorted, some of us have been getting rather hungry, sitting in this room on their own . . ."

Maddy took the hint. "Would you like me to see if there's some chicken in the fridge?"

Greykin's golden eyes gleamed. "Chicken would be most acceptable, or maybe even a tasty . . ."

"Bit of bacon!" Maddy and Rachel chorused with a grin.

A smile crossed Greykin's face. "Exactly!" he said.

That night, Maddy sat in bed with Greykin's small weight perched warmly on her knee. The tiny cat purred like a motor as she stroked his grey fur with her finger. "Oh Greykin, I'm *so* glad we're friends again," said Maddy softly. "It was awful when you were cross with me."

Greykin blinked up at her with his golden eyes. "I was worried, not cross," he said. "The magic is so important, Maddy! I know that it's not always easy, but . . ."

Maddy's finger stilled. "Then you *do* understand! I thought you didn't – I was feeling really hurt," she admitted, her cheeks turning pink.

Greykin rubbed his head against her finger, encouraging her to begin stroking him again. "Of course I understand. The magic is a very heavy responsibility, Maddy. It's not always enjoyable to have to do what it asks of you."

"No, it definitely isn't!" agreed Maddy. She let out a breath. "But Greykin, I've learned my lesson now – I really have. This all happened because I wanted to be part of Esme's crowd, and was pretending to be someone I wasn't. From now on, I'm just going to be myself."

Greykin beamed at her, his eyes full of warmth. "An excellent resolution! And who would *yourself* be, may I ask?"

Maddy grinned. "*Myself* is someone who has magical cats, and is the luckiest girl in the entire world!"

She scooped Greykin up in her hand, cuddling the tiny cat against her cheek. "I'll never forget it again," she whispered. "I missed you so much!"

Greykin stretched up on his hind legs, nuzzling his face against Maddy's cheek. "I missed you too," he said. "And you know, I think we three cats are rather lucky as well – we've got you!"

Even with her new power, Maddy felt very nervous when she arrived at school on Monday morning. How was Esme going to react when she discovered her skateboard was missing? Even worse, what if she somehow realized that Maddy was the one who'd taken it?

When she went into the classroom, she saw Esme hanging up her coat.

"Hi, Mads!" Esme nodded towards a couple of bags hanging on her peg. Maddy could just make out a skateboard shape inside the top one. "We're going to have some fun today!"

A prickle of dread swept through Maddy as Esme went into the classroom. Rachel came in, and Maddy pulled her over to one side. "Have you decided how you're going to keep Esme out of the way during break?" she hissed.

"Yes, I've got it all worked out," Rachel whispered back. "I'm going to ask her and the others to come and check out the science club."

Maddy's jaw dropped as she gaped at her friend in horror. "The *science* club? But they'll never want to do that, not in a million years!"

Rachel rolled her eyes good-naturedly. "It's not all Bunsen burners and lab coats, you know. It's going to be really fun. You just wait, I'll ask them now." And she headed off into the classroom.

Maddy trailed behind her, dreading what Esme's reaction to this was going to be. But to her surprise, Esme and the others started to smile as Rachel talked to them, and then to grin. Soon the little group was nodding enthusiastically.

Maddy stared. *What* had Rachel told them? Before she could go across and ask, Mr Orwell came into the room. "Take your seats, everyone," he called.

"Are they really going?" whispered Maddy as she sat down beside

Rachel at their table.

Rachel nodded. "I told you!"

"But how—"

"Quiet, girls," called Mr Orwell.

Maddy blew out a breath. Oh well, at least she knew Esme was taken care of! She kept a close eye on the clock, nervously waiting for the time to come.

Finally the bell rang, and Esme jumped to her feet. "Where do we have to go, Rachel?"

"To Class 5A's room," Rachel told her.

As Esme and the others went out, talking and laughing, Maddy caught Rachel's eye. "Are you going to tell me how you managed that?" she asked.

"Easy!" said Rachel with a

smile. "When Mrs Pratt and I were looking on the internet for science experiments, she found one which showed how to make lipglosses."

Maddy stared. "Lipglosses!"

Rachel nodded. "I told you science was fun. In science club we're going to learn how to make bath bombs and slime, invisible ink and model houses with lights that really work. It's going to be amazing! Anyway, the lipgloss experiment is a bit tricky so Mrs Pratt and I are going to try it out this break time to see if it works. I asked Esme and the others if they'd like to help."

Maddy grinned. "You're brilliant," she said warmly.

"See you later – and good luck!" said Rachel, squeezing her arm. She headed after the others to class 5A.

Maddy hung back, gazing at Esme's
bag hanging up in the cloakroom.
She took a shaky breath. What if she
popped back into view again, the
way she had with her dad? Imagine if
someone caught her stealing Esme's
skateboard!

Greykin? she thought nervously,
touching the tiny cat in her pocket.

To her relief she heard his soothing

voice in her mind as he rubbed his
nose against her finger. *You can do it,
Maddy! Just concentrate*.

I will, Maddy assured him, feeling
slightly better. She shut her eyes. *Cat
stealth*, she thought. *Cat* . . .

"Come along, Maddy. Get your
snack and out you go – it's lovely
and sunny out there," said Mr Orwell,
coming back in. Maddy started as
her eyes flew open. With Mr Orwell
watching, she had no choice but to get
her break-time apple from her bag and
go outside.

Leaving the room after her, Mr
Orwell shut the door and headed
towards the staff room. Maddy
checked around cautiously. There was
no one nearby; everyone had headed
out to the main playground. Taking a

deep breath, Maddy closed her eyes again.

Cat stealth . . . cat stealth . . .

The familiar magic prickled through her, growing and growing just like before. Her toes barely touching the ground, Maddy slipped unseen into the cloakroom. It was the work of a second to grab Esme's bag holding the skateboard from her peg, and then creep out again.

So far so good . . . but now what? She had to hide it somewhere it

wouldn't be found! Hugging the bag
to her chest, Maddy's gaze fell on the
fence that separated the playground
from the car park. On one side of the
car park was a small summerhouse on
a grass bank, where they sometimes
sat for painting lessons in the
summer. Perfect! She could hide the
skateboard there until the end of the
day.

With her cat powers surging
through her, Maddy cleared the fence
in a single leap and then made her

 way stealthily to the
summerhouse. Once
inside, she slipped the
skateboard under a
bench.

Hearing the bell
ring, Maddy's heart

somersaulted. Help! She had to get
back! Darting across the car park, she
sprang over the fence again. Luckily
everyone else was lining up in the
main part of the playground, and
no one noticed her. Letting her cat
powers fade, Maddy ran at normal
speed to join the rest of 6A.

Rachel moved to stand beside her.
"Did you do it?" she asked, her eyes
gleaming.

Maddy nodded. Just a few places
ahead of them in the line, Esme and
the others were comparing their little
pots of brightly-coloured lipgloss.

Esme turned to smile at Rachel.
"You know, that was a really cool way
to spend break. I thought science club
would be boring, but I was totally
wrong."

"Yeah," Jasmine agreed. "I'd like to
do that again sometime."

Rachel smiled back, looking
pleased. "You know, maybe they're
not so bad after all," she whispered to
Maddy as they headed inside.

Surprised pleasure flowed through
Maddy. If Rachel and Esme could
start getting on, that would be
amazing! Then she tensed as they all
trooped into the cloakroom. Esme

stopped dead by her peg. "It's gone!"

"What?" Jasmine was beside her.

"My skateboard," Esme hissed in dismay. "It's gone!"

"It can't have just gone," protested Mia.

"It has!" Esme looked around frantically. "It was in a bag on my peg, and now it's gone."

Jasmine, Mia and Sadie began to help her look as everyone else headed into the classroom. Maddy hastily started to search too, so it didn't seem suspicious.

"I can't believe it! Someone must have stolen it!" cried Esme.

"I'm sure it'll turn up," said Maddy weakly. At least Esme didn't seem to suspect her.

"Yes, someone probably just took it

for a joke," put in Rachel.

"Some joke!" snapped Esme. She stood with her hands on her hips, glaring at her peg.

"Rachel's right. I bet one of the boys just took it for a laugh," said Jasmine. "What a pain, though. You won't be able to do the dare now!"

Yes! thought Maddy, catching Rachel's eye.

Esme huffed out a breath and turned away from the peg. "Oh, don't worry, I'm still doing the dare."

An icy prickle ran over Maddy's scalp. "But – how can you without a skateboard?" she gasped.

"I'll just change to Plan B," said Esme smugly.

"Plan B?" echoed Rachel, her eyes wide.

162

Esme nodded. "I thought this morning that it might be even *more* daring to hitch a ride on my Rollerblades," she explained. "So I brought them along too." She pointed at the other bag on her peg. "I'll just use them instead!"

Chapter Eight

Maddy stared at the other bag in horror. Oh, why hadn't she checked it when she took the skateboard? Just then Mr Orwell stuck his head into the cloakroom, motioning impatiently. "Sit down, girls, and get your maths books out."

All through the maths lesson, Maddy found it impossible to concentrate. Surely Esme wasn't really about to do this mad dare?

Checking the clock, she swallowed hard. The school lunch van must just be arriving! She cast a nervous glance at Esme, and saw that she was looking at the clock too.

Esme put up her hand.

"Yes, Esme?" Mr Orwell looked up from marking Mia's worksheet.

"Can I go to the toilet, please?"

He nodded.

Double Dare

Maddy's heart plummeted as Esme headed into the cloakroom. This must be it! She had no idea how Esme was planning to do the dare, but she couldn't let her out of her sight. Her own hand shot into the air.

"Yes, Maddy?" Mr Orwell sighed.

"Can I go to the toilet too, please?" asked Maddy quickly.

"No. Wait until Esme gets back. I'm fed up of you girls messing around in there."

"But – but I really need to go!" she blurted out. Some of the boys sniggered, and Maddy's cheeks flamed red.

"No, Maddy. Just wait a few minutes until Esme gets back."

He turned away. Maddy's stomach churned. She could feel the time slipping by. Where was Esme? Oh, she couldn't bear this. "Please, Mr Orwell!" she burst out. "I really need . . ."

Her voice was cut off by the loud sound of the fire bell. The whole class jumped.

"It's the fire alarm!" exclaimed Jasmine.

Everyone's voices rose in an excited chatter. Maddy and Rachel stared at each other. *Oh no*! thought Maddy. It was Esme – this was how she was planning to stay away from the classroom long enough to do the dare!

Mr Orwell looked worried. "We weren't due a fire practice today. OK, everyone. Line up by the door quickly and quietly."

He strode to the cloakroom. "Esme!"

Double Dare

"Here, Mr Orwell," she appeared innocently in the doorway with one hand behind her back, but Mr Orwell was too distracted to notice.

"Great. All of you outside."

As Class 6A hurried outside along with the rest of the school, Maddy saw that Esme had the bag behind her back. The playground was chaos. It was so early in the term that none of the Reception children had ever done a fire drill before. Some of them seemed to think it was an extra playtime, and had raced away to the swings and slide. Others were crying at the loud noise, and the teachers were trying to round them up and comfort them.

"You lot stay here in line," Mr Orwell told 6A. "I'd better go and help."

"We'll help too, sir!" called Nathan
and some of the other boys, nudging
each other. The next second they were
racing away too.

"No! Come back!" Mr Orwell
called after them, but they ignored
him. Scraping his hands through his
hair, he set off after them. "Boys!"

Half of the rest of Class 6A saw

their opportunity and ran off too,
grinning. Maddy looked around
frantically. Where was Esme? There
was no sign of her anywhere! Her
heart thumping, Maddy raced round
the side of the building. *Think cat!* As
her powers surged through her, she
cleared the fence to the car park, and
stopped short in horror.

The school lunch van was just about
to leave. The men who delivered
the school lunches had shut the
double doors at the back and were
getting into the cab. Esme had her
Rollerblades on, and was crouching
behind one of the nearby cars. She
was really about to do it!

Maddy raced forward. "Esme!" she

said, reaching her side in just a few seconds.

Esme blinked. "Maddy! Where did you come from?"

Maddy ignored the question. Her cat's whiskers were tingling like mad. "You can't do this dare!"

"Of course I'm going to do it. I know I'm going to get into loads of trouble for smashing the fire alarm, so it had better be worth it! Go and get the others to come and see."

Maddy shook her head. "No."

Esme frowned. "No?" she echoed in astonishment. "Maddy, I said go and get the others!"

Fear pounded through Maddy. She knew that Esme was going to be furious with her – she probably wouldn't be her friend ever again.

But the words burst out of her
anyway. "I'm not going to get them,
and you're not going to do this
dare!"

Esme's mouth gaped open. "I'm
sorry?"

"You heard what I said. This is
stupid, Esme!"

"Like I'm going to listen to you!"
Esme snorted. The van engine fired up
and suddenly Esme skated away.

"No," Maddy gasped as Esme
grabbed the handle at the back of
the van.

The van started to move off. A
triumphant smile flashed across
Esme's face. "Woo-hoo!" she yelled
as it got faster, towing her along.

But suddenly her triumph turned
to a look of alarm. She tugged at her

arm. Maddy felt a stab of horror. One
of Esme's bracelets had slipped down
and caught on the handle, trapping
her. There was no way she could let

go of the van! Esme tried to tug her arm away, but couldn't. The van was going faster now, hurtling down the drive with Esme being pulled along behind it, struggling to keep her balance.

"Argh!" she shrieked, but the men didn't hear her.

"Esme!" Maddy cried. She ran after the van, her cat powers sweeping through her. The tarmac flashed by under her feet. Within a few seconds she had reached Esme's side. She saw the terror on the other girl's face.

"Maddy! Help!" she cried, too scared to wonder how it could be possible that Maddy was there.

Maddy's cat vision snapped into laser-sharp focus as she ran. All her attention seemed to zoom in on

the red bracelet hooked round the
door handle. An electric tingling
jabbed the tips of her fingers. It was
almost as if she was growing claws!
Acting instinctively, she sliced her
hand down like a cat's paw with
claws unsheathed. The bracelet
sheared apart. With a yell, Esme fell
sideways.

Maddy's cat powers couldn't help

her catch someone as they fell, but
her human instincts kicked in and
she grabbed Esme in her arms. They
tumbled to the ground together,
cushioning each other as they rolled
over and over.

The fall broke Maddy's

concentration, and her cat powers vanished. She sat up shakily, quickly checking in her pocket for Greykin. To her relief, the tiny cat was in his ceramic form, and seemed fine. "Esme? Are you OK?" she asked.

Esme pushed herself up. "Yes, I think so," she said weakly. She had a scratch on her face and a graze on her arm, but apart from that she was unharmed. Esme gazed at her wrist where her bracelet had been, and then at Maddy's face. "You saved me! But how did you catch up with me? How?" She stared at Maddy incredulously.

"I don't know. I just did," Maddy said. "I'm a fast runner, you know that."

"Yes, but . . ." Esme shook her head

wonderingly. "Well . . . wow!"

Maddy got to her feet and helped her up. "I'm really glad you're not hurt."

Esme shivered. "Imagine what would have happened if you hadn't saved me!" Both girls were quiet for a moment. Esme looked down, and to Maddy's surprise, tears filled her eyes. "I was so stupid," she burst out. "That was a mad thing to do. I should have listened to you when you tried to stop me."

Maddy squeezed her arm. "It's OK. Just don't do any more dares after this!"

Esme hesitated, biting her lip. "But . . . if I don't, then people won't like me."

Maddy gaped at her. "What are you

on about? Everyone likes you!"

Esme swallowed, and shook her head. "No, they – they only like me because I do dares and play tricks."

"That's not true!" exclaimed Maddy. "Jasmine and the others like the dares, but they'd like you even if you didn't do them." She studied the tall girl's face. "I mean it."

"Really?" Esme said tentatively.

"Really," Maddy assured her. She shook her head. "I can't believe you're even worried about it! Why?"

Esme took a breath. "I . . . I wasn't popular at my old school," she confided. "I used to get teased. I had short hair and I was good at sports, so lots of the other girls used to tease me and say I was a boy." She swallowed. "So when I moved house and school . . ."

"You decided to change yourself," Maddy finished for her. Suddenly it all made sense. The photos of Esme looking like a boy, the fact that she hadn't wanted to join the sports club at school, the dare game she'd been playing to make people think she was fun.

Esme nodded sheepishly. "It was

dumb of me. I just really wanted to be popular."

Maddy hesitated. It might have been silly of Esme, but she knew that she'd been just the same. She'd been so keen to hang round with the popular crowd that she'd acted in ways that weren't really her, not deep down. "I don't think it was that dumb," she said softly. "So was it all just pretend?"

"No," Esme said quickly. "I do like my hair like this, and I like make-up and music and playing dares. I just took it too far, I guess." She sighed. "And I wish I hadn't pretended I didn't like sport. I've been really missing it."

"You should join the sports club, then," Maddy said.

"But what will the others say?"

"They'll still be your friends,"
Maddy said, and she was sure it was
true.

"Will you?" Esme asked.

"Of course!" Maddy assured her.

Esme grinned with relief. "You're
really cool, Maddy."

Maddy shook her head and grinned
back. "Oh, I'm not," she said. "I'm
really not. But that's OK." She
touched the hard ceramic body of
Greykin in her pocket. She had
Rachel and she had magic in her life.
Suddenly she felt very happy just to
be her!

Esme took off her skates. "We
should get back and join the others. I
hope no one's noticed we're missing.
Are you OK?"

"I'm fine," Maddy said. And she

was. There wasn't a scratch on her. She wondered if it was more cat magic. Thinking back to how her fingers had tingled, she glanced down at her hands, remembering the strange feeling of claws. Cat magic really was amazing!

They headed back across the car park. Although it felt like they had been gone ages, they could still hear the whistles and the teachers shouting.

"I guess I'm going to be in trouble for setting off the fire alarm," Esme sighed.

Maddy gave her a sympathetic look as they climbed the fence. She had a feeling Esme was right, but even cat magic couldn't prevent that! "Maybe it won't be too bad," she said.

"Well, you're right about one thing

– that's the last dare I'm ever going to do!" Esme declared. "Come on!" She broke into a jog.

Maddy hung back as a purr vibrated

against her leg. Greykin! The problem he had come to life to deal with had finally been solved. But the relief she felt was tempered by a twisting in her heart. Now that the job was done, it would be time to say goodbye.

Just remember. As one adventure ends, another begins, Greykin's warm voice purred in her head.

Maddy smiled. *I know*. And holding tight to that thought, she ran to join the others.

After school, Maddy sat on the chair in her room, stroking the little grey cat as he wound in and out of her fingers.

"You did exceptionally well today, Maddy," he said. "Esme might have been seriously hurt, but for you."

"And now the dares have stopped
for good," said Maddy in relief.

Esme had bravely confessed to
Mr Orwell about setting off the fire
alarm. And though he'd given her a
week's detention for the prank, he'd
been kind too, and had suggested that
she join some of the clubs to help
her settle in. Esme had accepted with
delight. She'd decided to join the
sports club. Jasmine was going to as

well, and all of them were planning on joining the science club when that started – much to Rachel's delight!

"I hope Esme'll be happier now," said Maddy.

"I'm sure she will." Greykin's voice was wise. "She's learned to be true to herself, and to trust that others will like her for who she really is. That's a valuable lesson indeed, isn't it?" He smiled at Maddy, and she smiled sheepishly back, remembering that Esme wasn't the only one who'd had to learn this!

She stroked the little cat in silence for a few moments, her throat tightening.

Greykin had been here for over a week, and so much of that time had been spent with them hardly talking! And now he was going away, and it might be months and months before she saw him again.

Maddy swallowed hard. "I . . . I wish you didn't have to leave, Greykin," she said in a small voice.

"I, too, wish I could stay," Greykin replied. "But the others, I believe, would object." He shot an amused look at the other two cats on Maddy's desk – slim black Nibs, and cheeky tabby Ollie. "And besides, you may feel that you'd rather have some of their powers instead of mine." He raised an eyebrow, but she could see the teasing glint in his eye.

"No, I don't," said Maddy, suddenly

close to tears. "Oh, Greykin, please don't go! I'm really going to miss you."

"I'll miss you too," he said gently. "But it's only for a while, and then I'll return." Rising up on his hind legs, Greykin hooked his paws around her thumb in a tiny feline embrace. "Goodbye for now, Maddy."

Swallowing hard, Maddy kissed the tip of her finger and touched his head. "Goodbye," she managed.

Greykin dropped back to the desk with a small *thump*. With a final loving smile, he slipped into place between the other two cats.

Maddy watched as a faint shimmer seemed to pass over him . . . and then his soft fur became hard and ceramic once more. The three cats nestled together. Letting out a breath, Maddy carefully stroked their cool heads. The magic was over for now. But not for ever.

"What will my next adventure be?" she whispered to them.

All three cats seemed to smile.

THE END

About the author

Kitty Wells is the pen-name for Lee Weatherly. Lee was born in Little Rock, Arkansas, USA and now lives in Hampshire with her husband. Lee's first book for children, *Child X*, was published by David Fickling Books in June 2002. It was shortlisted for the Red House Children's Book Award, the Sheffield Book Award and the Leicester Book Award. Lee has written three more books for older children for DFB, and is also the author of Bloomsbury's *Glitterwings Academy* series for younger children.

Lee has always adored cats, so writing

the *Pocket Cats* series is her dream job. She owns a huge tabby cat called Bernard, and when they met it was love at first sight. Bernard makes a funny chirruping noise like a pigeon and his favourite toy is a laser-light that he chases around the room, although he gets very cross when he can't catch it!

***Don't miss the
first three
brilliant books in the
Pocket Cats series!***

Join Maddy as she meets Greykin, Nibs
and Ollie for the very first time. She really
is the luckiest girl in the world! But being
the owner of the magical Pocket Cats is a
serious job, and as each cat comes to life
Maddy has a new problem to solve. It's
a good thing she's got the Pocket Cats on
her side!

More **Pocket Cats**
adventures

Magical Mayhem

by Kitty Wells

Maddy could never have guessed that one day she'd be helping a ghost! But she and Nibs have to find a way to solve the spook's problem before things get out of control!

More **Pocket Cats**
adventures

Friends Forever

by Kitty Wells

When not one, not two, but all THREE of the Pocket Cats come to life, Maddy can't imagine anything better. Until she finds herself facing the most difficult decision of all . .